ABOUT THE AUTHOR

Christopher Pike was born in New York, but grew up in
Los Angeles, where he lives to this day. Prior to becoming a
writer he worked in a factory, painted houses and
programmed computers. His hobbies include astronomy,
meditating, running and making sure his books are
prominently displayed in his local bookshop. As well as
being a bestselling children's writer, he is also the author of
THE SEASON OF PASSAGE, THE COLD ONE and
THE LISTENERS for adults.

Spooksville

Spooksville
THE SECRET PATH

Christopher Pike

*Hodder
Children's
Books*

a division of Hodder Headline plc

First published in the USA in 1995
by Pocket Books

First Published in Great Britain in 1995
by Hodder Children's Books

10 9 8

A Catalogue record for this book is available from the British Library

ISBN 0-340-66113-5

Typeset by Avon Dataset Ltd, Bidford-on-Avon

Printed and bound in Great Britain by
Cox & Wyman Ltd, Reading, Berks

Hodder and Stoughton
a division of Hodder Headline plc
338 Euston Road
London NW1 3BH

One

For Adam Freeman, moving to Spooksville wasn't something he'd planned. But being only twelve, he hadn't a lot to say in the matter. They had to move, his parents said, because of his father's job. Of course, when they told him about Spooksville, they didn't call it that. Springville was the proper name of the small oceanside town. It was only the local kids who called it by the scarier, but more accurate, title. It was only kids who knew how weird the place could get after dark.

Or even during the day.

That was the thing about Spooksville.

Not all its monsters waited until the sun went down to appear.

As he unpacked the removal van and carried his stuff up to his new room, Adam didn't believe in monsters or the supernatural. But that was soon to change. Oh, yes, in a big way.

'Adam,' his father called from inside the truck. 'Can you give me a hand with this love seat?'

'Sure,' Adam replied, setting down the box of clothes he was carrying. He enjoyed helping, even though his muscles were still sore from loading the truck two days ago in Kansas City, Missouri. His father, who was something of a nerd, had driven straight through to the West Coast town. Adam had slept on a rubber mat in the back of the truck. The road had been rough.

Adam was small for his age, but he was growing steadily and figured he'd catch up soon. The problem was he had no one in particular to catch up to now that all his friends were over a thousand miles away. Adam thought of Sammy and Mike as he climbed into the truck. He wondered what they were doing right now. His father paused to stare at him.

'What's that look?' his dad asked. 'Are you homesick already?'

Adam shrugged. 'I'm OK.'

His dad ruffled his hair. 'Don't worry. You'll make new friends soon. Not all the cool guys live in the Midwest.' He smiled as he added, 'Not all the cool girls live there, either.'

Adam frowned as he leaned over to pick up his end of the short sofa. 'I'm not interested in girls. And they're definitely not interested in me.'

'It's when you're not interested in them that they start to chase you.'

'Is that true?'

'Some of the time, if you're lucky.' His father leaned over and picked up his end. 'Let's lift on the count of three. One – two – '

'Why is it called a love seat?' Adam asked. He was curious about many things, even things he pretended to have no interest in.

'Because it's only big enough to fit two lovers. Are you ready? One – two – '

'You know I didn't really know any girls in Kansas City,' Adam added hastily.

His father stood up again and stretched. 'What about Denise? You saw her all the time.'

Adam felt his cheeks redden. 'Yes. But she was just a friend. She wasn't a . . .' He struggled to find the right word. 'She wasn't a *girl* girl.'

'Thank God for that.' His father leaned over again. 'Let's just lift this thing and get it over with. One – two – '

'Three!' Adam said as he yanked up hard, catching his father by surprise.

'Ahh!' his father exclaimed and dropped his end. He clutched his lower back and his face twisted with pain.

'Did you hurt yourself?' Adam asked, thinking that it was a stupid question. His father waved him away as he limped down the ramp of the truck.

'I'm all right. Don't worry. Just a pulled muscle. We need a break anyway.'

'I'm sorry.'

'It wasn't your fault.'

Adam was concerned. 'Are you sure you're all right?' His father wasn't exactly in perfect shape. In the last couple of years he had grown a fair-sized belly. Too many doughnuts and sodas, Adam thought, even though those were two of his favourite foods, too. That was one of the things that made his dad sort of a nerd – he liked junk food as much as kids.

'I'm fine,' his dad said. 'Let's stop and have a drink. What would you like?'

'A Coke,' Adam replied, following him down the ramp.

'I don't think we have any Coke in the refrigerator.'

'I don't think we have a fridge,' Adam said. He pointed to the large white container at the rear of the van. 'We haven't unloaded it yet.'

'Good point,' his father said, sitting down on the lawn.

'Should I tell Mum you're hurt?'

'Leave her, she's busy.' He pulled a twenty dollar bill from his back pocket and handed it to Adam. 'Why don't you run down to the 7-Eleven on the corner and get us a cold six-pack.'

Adam pocketed the note. 'Yeah, I'll just tell them I forgot my ID, but I really am over twenty-one.'

'I meant a six-pack of Coke.'

'I know.' Adam turned away. 'I'll be back in a few minutes.'

His dad groaned as he leaned back on his elbows and stared up at the sky. 'Take your time. I don't think I'll be going anywhere anytime soon.'

Two

It was while Adam was returning from the store with the sodas that he met Sally Wilcox. She sneaked up on him from behind. A pretty girl about his age, she had long brown hair and a stick-like figure that somehow made her look like a doll that a fairy queen had brought to life with the wave of a magic wand. It was a hot day, and her long legs beneath her white shorts were tanned and bony. She had the widest brown eyes Adam had ever seen, and she didn't look a thing like Denise back in Missouri.

'Hello,' she said. 'Are you the new kid in town?'

'I suppose so. I just got here.'

She stuck out her hand. 'My name's Sara Wilcox, but you can call me Sally. It's easier to remember.'

Adam took her hand. 'I'm Adam Freeman.'

Sally practically shook his fingers off. 'What should I call you?'

'Adam.'

She nodded at his Coke cans. 'Are those cold?'

'Yes.'

'May I have one, please?'

It wasn't as if he could say no, being the new kid and all. He gave her a Coke, which she promptly opened and drank. She didn't even let out a loud burp afterwards. Adam was impressed.

'You must have been thirsty,' he remarked.

'I was.' She studied him for a moment. 'You look depressed, Adam.'

'Huh?'

'You look sad. Are you sad?'

He shrugged. 'No.'

Sally nodded to herself. 'You left someone special behind. I understand.'

Adam blinked. 'What are you talking about?' This girl was weird.

Sally waved her hand as if what she was saying was obvious. 'You don't have to be embarrassed. You're a good-looking guy. You must have had a good-looking girlfriend wherever you came from.' She paused. 'Where was that anyway?'

'Kansas City.'

Sally nodded sympathetically. 'She's a long way away now.'

'Who?'

'I just met you, Adam. How would I know her name?'

Adam frowned. 'My best friends in Kansas City were named Sammy and Mike.'

Sally tossed her long hair impatiently. 'If you don't want to talk about her, that's OK. I'm going through an identity crisis myself. But you couldn't tell that just by looking at me, could you?'

'No.'

'I hide it. I suffer in silence. It's better that way. It builds character. My aunt says I have a face full of character. Do you think that's true?'

Adam resumed walking towards his house. The Cokes were getting warm and Sally was making him dizzy. But it had been nice of her to say he was good-looking. Adam was a little insecure about his looks. His brown hair, similar in colour to Sally's, was not nearly so long. His father cut his hair, and the man believed in closely trimmed heads as well as lawns. Nor was Adam as tall as Sally, who seemed to him to have stilts sewn on to her legs. But people told him he had a handsome face. At least his mother did when she was in a good mood.

'I guess,' he replied to her last question about the character in her face.

She followed him. 'Are you going to introduce me to your family? I always like to meet parents. You can get a good idea of what a guy is going to become by looking at his dad.'

'I hope not,' Adam muttered.

'What did you say?'

'Nothing. How long have you been living here?'

'Twelve years. All my life. I'm one of the lucky ones.'

'You mean, it's really neat living in Springville?'

'No. I mean I'm lucky to be alive still. Not all kids last twelve years in Spooksville.'

'What's Spooksville?'

Sally spoke in a serious tone. 'It's where you're living now, Adam. Only adults call it Springville. Kids know the real story of this place. And let me tell you it deserves to be called Spooksville.'

Adam was bewildered. 'But why?'

She leaned close, as though telling him a great secret. 'Because people here disappear. Usually kids like us. No one knows where they go, and no one talks about the fact that they're gone. Because they're all too afraid.'

Adam smiled uneasily. 'Are you pulling my leg?'

Sally stood back. 'If I was pulling your leg, you wouldn't

be standing. I'm telling you the straight truth. This town is dangerous. My advice to you is to drive out of here before the sun goes down.' Sally paused and put a hand on his shoulder. 'Not that I want to see you leave.'

Adam shook his head. 'I'm not leaving. I don't believe a whole town can be spooked. I don't believe in vampires and werewolves and junk like that. I'm surprised you do.' He added quietly, 'I think you *are* going through an identity crisis.'

Sally pulled back her hand and regarded him gravely as she spoke. 'Let me tell you the story of Leslie Lotte before you decide I'm crazy. Until a month ago, she lived down the block from me. She was cute. You might have been interested in her if you had met her before me. Anyway, she was great at making stuff: jewellery, clothes, kites. She was really into kites. Don't ask me why. Maybe she wanted to be a bird when she grew up. Anyway she used to fly her kites in the park by the cemetery. Yeah, that's right. In Spooksville the park is next to the cemetery, which is next to the witch's castle – which is a story in itself. Leslie used to go to the park by herself, even close to dark. I told her not to. Last month she was there all alone flying her kite when a huge gust of wind came along and blew her into the sky. Blew her right into a dark cloud, which swallowed her whole. Can you believe that?'

'No.'

Sally was exasperated. 'I'm not lying. I may be confused about my personal values at the moment, but the truth is still very important to me.'

'If she was flying the kite all alone in the park, how do you know what happened to her? Who told you?'

'Watch.'

'Who's Watch?'

'You'll meet him. And before you get worried, I want you to know that our relationship is not and never has been romantic. We're just good friends.'

'I'm not worried, Sally.'

She hesitated. 'Good. Watch saw Leslie disappear into the sky. He wasn't in the park but in the cemetery. So you see, technically, Leslie was in the park all alone.'

'It sounds to me like your friend Watch has a vivid imagination.'

'That's true. He can't see very well, either. But he's not a liar.'

'What was he doing in the cemetery?'

'Oh, he hangs out there a lot. He's one of the few kids who lives here who enjoys Spooksville. He loves mystery and adventure. If he wasn't so weird I'd be attracted to him.'

'I like mystery and adventure,' Adam said proudly.

Sally wasn't impressed. 'Then you can camp out in the cemetery with Watch and tell me what it's like.' She stuck out her arm, pointing. 'That's not your house down the street with that chubby nerd on the front lawn?'

'Yes, and that chubby nerd is my father.'

Sally put her hands to her mouth. 'Oh, no.'

'He's not that bad,' Adam said defensively.

'No. I'm not upset about your father's appearance, although you're going to have to watch your diet and the TV shows you watch as you get older. It's your house that's no good.'

'What's wrong with it? Don't tell me someone was murdered there?'

Sally shook her head. 'They weren't murdered.'

'Well, that's a relief.'

'They killed themselves.' Sally nodded seriously. 'It was an old couple. No one knows why they did it. They must have been going through an identity crisis. They just hanged themselves from the chandelier.'

'We don't have a chandelier.'

'They were fat old people. The chandelier broke when they strung themselves up with the ropes. Someone told me they didn't leave any money for a proper funeral. Their bodies are supposed to be buried in your basement.'

'We don't have a basement.'

Sally nodded. 'The police had to fill it in, in case you found the bodies.'

Adam sighed. 'Oh brother. Do you want to meet my father?'

'Yes. Just don't ask me to stay for lunch. I'm a picky eater.'

'Somehow I'm not surprised,' Adam said.

Three

His mum and dad were very impressed with Sally, Adam was surprised to see. Of course, Sally kept her remarks to a minimum and her identity crisis private while she spoke to them. Sally did not have an opportunity to meet Claire, Adam's seven-year-old sister, because she was asleep on the floor in one of the back bedrooms. His father hadn't set up the beds yet. From the way he was hobbling around supporting his lower back as if he were a monkey with a sore tail, he looked like he needed one. His father winked at Adam and told him to go out and play with Sally. He said that neither of them would be doing any more heavy lifting that day.

Adam didn't know what the wink was supposed to mean.

He wasn't interested in Sally. Not as a girlfriend.

He had no desire to have a girlfriend before seventh grade.

But school didn't start for another three months, so he had a whole summer full of monsters to look forward to.

Not that he believed a word Sally had told him.

'Let me show you the town,' Sally said as they stepped out of his front door. 'But don't be deceived by what you see. This place looks perfectly normal, but it's not. For example, you might see a young mother walk by pushing her newborn infant. She might smile at you and say hello. She might look real, and her baby might look cute. But there's always the possibility that that young mother is responsible for the disappearance of Leslie Lotte, and that her baby is a robot.'

'I thought you said a cloud swallowed Leslie.'

'Yeah, but *who* was in the cloud? These are the kind of questions you have to ask yourself this afternoon as you check out the scene.'

Adam was getting weary of Sally's warnings. 'I don't believe in robots. There are no robots. That's a simple fact.'

Sally raised a know-it-all eyebrow. 'Nothing is simple in Spooksville.'

Springville – Adam refused to think of it by any other name – was tiny. Nestled between two gentle sets of hills on the north and south, it had the ocean to the west. To the east a range of rough hills rose sharply. Adam was inclined to call them mountains. Naturally, Sally said there were many bodies buried in those hills. Most of the town was set on a slope, that only levelled out as it neared the water. Close to the shore, at the end of a rocky point, stood a tall lighthouse that looked out over the hard blue water as if in search of adventure. Sally explained that the water in and around Springville wasn't safe, either.

'Lots of riptides and undertows,' she said. 'Sharks, too – great whites. I knew a guy – he was out on his boogie board only a hundred feet from the shore, and a shark swam by and bit his right leg off. Just like that. If you don't believe me, you can meet him. His name's David Green, but we call him Jaws.'

This story had a ring of truth to it, at least.

'I don't like to swim all that much,' Adam muttered.

Sally shook her head. 'You don't even have to go in the water to have problems. The crabs come right up on the sand to nibble on you.' She added, 'We don't have to go to the beach right now if you don't want to.'

'Another time might be better,' Adam agreed.

They did head in the direction of the water, though. Sally wanted to show him the arcade next to the cinema, which, she said, was owned by the local undertaker. Apparently it showed only horror movies. The cinema and the arcade were located next to the pier, which, Sally said, was about as safe as a single plank set above boiling lava. Along the way they passed a supermarket.

Parked in front was a black Corvette convertible, with the top down. Adam wasn't into cars, but he thought Corvettes were cool. They looked like rockets. He stared at the car as they strode by, for a moment blocking out Sally's rambling. Like so much of Springville, the supermarket was built on a hill. Adam was shocked to see that a shopping trolley had slipped loose from its place near the front doors and was heading for the car. He hated to think of such a beautiful car getting a dent in it, and jumped forward to stop the trolley. Sally screamed behind him.

'Adam!' she cried. 'Don't go near that car!'

But she was too late with her warning. He stopped the trolley only inches from the car door, feeling as if he had done his good deed for the day. He noticed that Sally was still standing where he'd left her. She seemed afraid to approach the vehicle. As he started to move the trolley to a safe place, a soft yet mysterious voice spoke at his back.

'Thank you, Adam. You have done your good deed for the day.'

He turned toward the most beautiful woman he'd ever seen. She was tall – most adults were. Her black hair was long and curly, her eyes so dark and big, they were like ghostly mirrors that opened only at night. Her face was very pale, white as a statue's, her lips as red as fresh blood. She wore a white dress that swept past her knees. In her hands she carried a small white purse. She must have been in her late twenties, but seemed ageless. It was a warm day, yet she had on gloves, as red as her lips. She smiled at his shocked expression.

'You wonder how I know your name,' she said. 'Isn't that so, Adam?'

He nodded, dumbstruck. She took a step closer.

'There isn't much that happens in this town that I don't know about,' she said. 'You just arrived today. Isn't that so?'

He found his voice. 'Yes, ma'am.'

She chuckled softly. 'How do you like Spooksville so far?'

He stuttered. 'I thought only kids called it Spooksville?'

She took another step forward. 'There are a few grown-ups who know its real name. You'll meet another one today. He'll tell you things you might not want to hear, but that will be up to you.' She glanced at her car, then at the shopping trolley still in his hand, and her smile broadened. 'I give you this warning because you have done me a favour this day, protecting my car. That was valiant of you, Adam.'

'Thank you, ma'am.'

She chuckled again. 'You have manners. That is rare among the young in this town.' She paused. 'Do you think that is one of the reasons they have so many – problems?'

Adam gulped. 'What kind of problems?'

The woman looked in the direction of Sally. 'I'm sure your friend has already told you many frightening things about this town. Don't believe half of them. Of course, the other half – you might want to believe.' She paused as if sharing a private joke with herself. Then she waved at Sally. 'Come here, child.'

Sally approached reluctantly, and then stood close to Adam. She was so close he noticed she was shaking. The woman studied her up and down and frowned.

'You don't like me,' she said finally.

Sally swallowed. 'We're just out walking.'

'You're just out talking.' She pointed a finger at Sally. 'You watch what you talk about. Every time you say my name, child, I hear it. And I remember. Do you understand?'

Sally was still shaking, but a sudden stubbornness hardened her features. 'I understand very well, thank you.'

'Good.'

'How's your castle keeping these days?' Sally asked sarcastically. 'Any cold drafts?'

The woman's frown deepened, then unexpectedly she

20

smiled. Adam would have said it was a cold smile if it hadn't been so enchanting. This woman held him spellbound.

'You're insolent, Sally,' she said. 'Which is good. I was insolent as a child' – she paused – 'until I learned better.' She glanced at Adam. 'You know I have a castle?'

'No, I didn't know,' Adam said. He liked castles, although he'd never seen one, much less been inside one.

'Would you like to visit me there someday?' the woman asked.

'No,' Sally said suddenly.

Adam glared at Sally. 'I can answer for myself,' he said.

Sally shook her head. 'You don't want to go there. Kids who go there, they—'

'They what?' the woman interrupted. Sally wouldn't look at her now, only at Adam. Sally seemed to back down.

'It's not a good idea to go there,' was all Sally said.

The woman reached out and touched the side of Adam's face. Her fingers were warm, soft – they didn't feel dangerous. Yet Adam trembled beneath them. The woman's eyes, as she stared at him, seemed to pierce to the centre of his brain.

'Nothing is the way it looks,' she said gently. 'Nobody is just one way. When you hear stories about me – perhaps from this skinny girl here, perhaps from others – know that they're only partially true.'

Adam had trouble speaking. 'I don't understand.'

'You will, soon enough,' the woman said. Her fingernails – they were quite long, and so red – brushed close to his eyes, almost touching his lashes. 'You have such nice eyes, did you know that, Adam?' She glanced over at Sally. 'And you have such a nice mouth.'

Sally gave a fake smile. 'I know that.'

The woman chuckled softly and drew back. Reaching out and opening her car door, she glanced back at them one last time. 'I'll will see both of you later – under different circumstances,' she said.

Then she got into her car, waved once, and drove away.

Sally was ready to throw a fit.

'Do you know who that was?' she exclaimed.

'No,' Adam said, still recovering from the shock of meeting the woman. 'She didn't tell me her name.'

'That was Ms Ann Templeton. She is the great-great-great-great-granddaughter of Mrs Madeline Templeton.'

'Who's that?'

'The woman who founded this town about two hundred years ago. A witch if ever there was one. Witchery runs in their family. The woman you just met is the most dangerous creature in all of Spooksville. Nobody knows how many kids she's killed.'

22

'She seemed nice.'

'Adam! She's a witch! There are no nice witches except in the *Wizard of Oz*. And one thing Spooksville sure doesn't have is a yellow brick road. You have to stay away from that woman or you'll end up as a frog chirping in the stagnant pond behind the cemetery.'

Adam had to shake himself to clear his brain. It was almost as if the woman had cast a spell on him. But a pleasant spell, one that made him feel warm inside.

'How did she know my name?' he muttered out loud.

Sally was exasperated. 'Because she's a witch! Get a grip on reality, would ya? She probably just had to look in a big pot filled with boiling livers and kidneys to know everything about you. Why, I wouldn't be surprised if she sent that shopping trolley flying toward her car just so you could run over and stop it. Just so she could stop and bewitch your tiny little mind. Are you listening to me, Mr Kansas City?'

Adam frowned. 'The trolley wasn't flying. It never left the ground.'

Sally raised her arms toward the sky. 'The kid has to see a broom fly across the moon before he'll believe in witches! Well, that's just great. Be that way. Get yourself changed into something gross and disgusting. I don't care. I have problems of my own.'

'Sally. Why are you always yelling at me?'

'Because I *care*. Now let's get out of here. Let's go to the arcade. It's pretty safe there.'

'None of the games are haunted?' Adam teased. Sally stopped to give him another one of her impatient looks.

'A *couple* of games are haunted,' she said. 'You can't put quarters in them. Of course, knowing you, you'll head straight for them.'

'I don't know,' Adam said. 'My dad wanted his change back from when I bought the Cokes. I don't have any money.'

'Then thank your dad for a small favour,' Sally said.

Four

They never got to the arcade. Instead they ran into Sally's friend, Watch. He was an interesting-looking fellow. About Sally's height, with blond hair the colour of the sun and arms that reached halfway to the ground. His ears were big. Adam saw in an instant where he got his nickname. On each arm he wore two large watches, four that Adam could see. Maybe he had a couple in his pockets that Adam didn't know about. The lenses on his glasses were thick – they could have been swiped from the ends of telescopes. Sally seemed happy to see him. She introduced Adam.

'Adam's from Kansas City,' she said to Watch. 'He just got here and is finding the change of scenery painful.'

Adam frowned. 'It's not that bad.'

'What are your favourite subjects in school?' Watch asked.

'Watch is a science nut,' Sally said. 'If you like science,

Watch will like you. Me, I don't care if you flunked biology. My love is unconditional.'

'I like science,' Adam said. He gestured to Watch's arms. 'Why do you wear so many watches? Isn't one enough?'

'I always like to know what time it is in each part of the country,' Watch said.

'There are four time zones in America,' Sally said.

'I know that,' Adam said. 'Kansas City is two time zones ahead of the West Coast. But why do you want to know what time it is in all these places?'

Watch lowered his head. 'Because my mother lives in New York. My sister lives in Chicago, and my father lives in Denver.' Watch shrugged. 'I like to know what time it is for each of them.'

There was sadness in Watch's voice as he spoke of his family. Adam felt he shouldn't ask why everyone was so spread out. Sally must have felt the same way. She spoke up again.

'I was just telling Adam how dangerous this town is,' she said. 'I don't think he believes me.'

'Did you really see Leslie Lotte get swallowed by a cloud?' Adam asked Watch.

Watch looked at Sally. 'What did you tell him?'

Sally was defensive. 'Just what you told me.'

Watch scratched his head. His blond hair was kind of

thin. 'I saw Leslie get lost in the fog. And then none of us could find her. But she might have run away from home.'

'The fog, a cloud – what's the difference?' Sally said. 'The sky ate her, it's as simple as that. Hey, Watch, what are you doing today? Do you want to go to the arcade with us?'

Watch brightened. 'I'm going to see the Bum. He's going to show me the Secret Path.'

Sally shuddered. 'You're not taking the Secret Path. You'll die.'

'Really?' Watch said.

'What's the Secret Path?' Adam asked.

'Don't tell him,' Sally said. 'He just got here. I like him, and I don't want him to die.'

'I don't think we'll die,' Watch said. 'But we might disappear.'

Adam was interested. He'd never disappeared before. 'How?' he asked.

Watch turned to Sally. 'Tell him about it,' he said.

Sally shook her head. 'It's too dangerous, and I'm responsible for him.'

'Who made you responsible?' Adam asked, getting annoyed. 'I'm my own person. You can't tell me what to do.' He turned to Watch. 'Tell me about the path. And tell me who Bum is.'

'Bum is the town bum,' Sally interrupted. 'He used to be the mayor until Ann Templeton, town witch, put a curse on him.'

'Is that true?' Adam asked Watch.

'Bum was the mayor,' Watch agreed. 'But I don't know if he became a bum because he got cursed. It may have been because he got lazy. He was always a lousy mayor.'

'What exactly is the Secret Path?' Adam asked again.

'We don't know,' Sally said. 'It's a secret.'

'Tell me what you do know,' Adam said, getting exasperated.

'There's supposed to be a special path that winds through town and leads into other dimensions,' Watch said. 'I've searched for it for years, but never found it. But Bum is supposed to know it.'

'Who says?' Adam asked.

'Bum says,' Watch said.

'Why is he going to tell you the secret?' Sally asked. 'Why today?'

Watch was thoughtful. 'I don't know. I gave him a sandwich last week. Maybe he just wants to thank me for it.'

'Maybe he wants to get you killed,' Sally grumbled.

'It wasn't that bad a sandwich,' Watch said.

'When you say the path leads into other dimensions,'

Adam said, 'what do you mean?'

'There is more than one Spooksville,' Sally said.

'Huh?' Adam said.

'This town overlaps with other realities,' Watch explained. 'Sometimes those other realities blur into this one.'

'That's why this is such a weird place to live,' Sally added.

Adam shook his head. 'Do you have any proof that these dimensions exist?'

'No direct proof,' Watch said. 'But a man on my block was supposed to have known about the Secret Path.'

'What did he say about it?' Adam asked.

'He disappeared before I could ask him.' Watch paused to check one of his watches. 'Bum is waiting for me. If you want to come, you have to decide now.'

'Don't go, Adam,' Sally pleaded. 'You're young. You have your whole future in front of you.'

Adam laughed at her concern. He was interested in the Secret Path, but he couldn't say he believed it really existed. 'I have a long boring day in front of me. I want to see what this is about.' He nodded to Watch. 'Let's go find this Bum.'

Five

Sally ended up going with them, complaining all the time about how they could get stuck in a black hole and squashed down to the size of ants. Adam and Watch ignored her.

They found Bum sitting by the pier on a concrete wall, feeding the birds from a nearby pile of seeds. On the way to the water Watch had stopped and bought a turkey sandwich at a deli as a gift. Bum accepted it hungrily and didn't even pause to look at them until he'd finished eating.

Bum was dirty with a long scraggly grey coat that looked as if it had been dug out of a rubbish bin. His face was unshaven, his cheeks stained with grease and dirt. His hair was the colour of used motor oil. He could have been sixty, but maybe cleaned up he would have looked closer to forty. Although thin, he had eyes that were exceptionally bright and alert. He didn't look drunk, just hungry.

Finished eating, he regarded them closely, searching Adam up and down.

'You're the new kid in town,' he said finally. 'I heard about you.'

'Really?' Adam said. 'Who told you about me?'

'I don't reveal my sources,' Bum replied, throwing the final crumbs from his sandwich to the birds that flocked around him as if he were Father Bird. Bum continued, 'Your name's Adam and you're from Kansas City.'

'That's right, sir,' Adam said.

Bum grinned wolfishly. 'No one calls me sir any more, kid. And to tell you the truth, I don't care. I'm Bum – that's my new name. Call me that.'

'Did you really used to be mayor?' Adam asked.

Bum stared out to sea. 'Yes. But that was long ago, when I was young and cared about being a big shot.' He shook his head and added, 'I was a lousy mayor.'

'I told him that,' Watch said.

Bum chuckled. 'I'm sure you did. Now, Watch, what do you want? The secret to the Secret Path? How do I know you're qualified to learn it?'

'What qualifications are necessary?' Watch asked.

Bum asked them to lean closer. He spoke in a confidential tone. 'You have to be fearless. If you walk the Secret Path and find the other towns, then fear is the one thing that can get you killed. But if you keep your head, think fast, you can survive the road. It's the only way.'

Adam had to draw in a breath. 'Have you taken the Secret Path?' he asked.

Bum laughed softly, mainly to himself. 'Many times, kid. I've taken it left and I've taken it right. I've even taken it straight up, if you know what I mean.'

'I don't,' Adam said honestly.

'The Secret Path doesn't always lead to the same place,' Bum said. 'It all depends on you. If you're a little scared, you end up in a place that's a little scary. If you're terrified, the path is like a road to terror.'

'Cool,' Watch said.

'Cool?' Sally said sarcastically. 'Who wants to be terrified? Come on, Adam, let's get out of here. Neither of us is qualified. We're both cowards.'

'Speak for yourself,' Adam said, getting more interested. Bum had a powerful way of speaking – it was hard to doubt his words. 'Can the path lead to wonderful places?' Adam asked.

'Oh, yes,' Bum said. 'But those are the hardest to reach. Only the best people get to them. Most just get stuck in twilight zone realms and are never heard from again.'

'That wouldn't bother me,' Watch said. 'I love that old show, *The Twilight Zone*. Please tell us the way.'

Bum studied each of them, and even though the smile left his mouth, it remained in his eyes. Adam liked him but wasn't sure if he was a good man. The words of Ann Templeton, supposed witch, came back to haunt him.

'There are a few grown-ups who know its real name. You'll meet another one today. He'll tell you things you might not want to hear, but that will be up to you. I give you this warning because you have done me a favour this day.'

'If I tell you the way,' Bum said, 'you have to promise not to tell anyone else.'

'Wait a second!' Sally exclaimed. 'I never said I wanted to know the secret.' She put her hands over her ears. 'This town is bad enough. I don't want to fall into a worse one.'

Bum chuckled. 'I know you, Sally. You're more curious than the other two. I've watched you this past year. You go out looking for the Secret Path all the time.'

Sally pulled down her hands. 'Never!'

'I've seen you searching for it,' Watch said.

'Only to block it up so that no one else can find it,' she said quickly.

'The Secret Path cannot be blocked up,' Bum said, and now he sounded serious. 'It's ancient. It existed before this town was built, and it will continue to exist after this town has turned to dust. No one walks it and remains the

34

same. If you choose to take it, you must know there is no going back. The path is dangerous, but if your heart remains strong, the rewards can be great.'

'Could we find some treasure?' Adam asked, getting more excited. Bum stared him right in the eye.

'You might find wealth beyond your imagination,' Bum said.

Sally brightened. 'I could use a few bucks.'

Bum threw his head back and laughed. 'You three are a team, I see that already. All right, I'll tell you the secret. After you promise to keep it secret.'

'We promise,' they said together.

'Good.' Bum asked them to come close again, and he lowered his voice to a whisper. 'Follow the life of the witch. Follow her all the way to her death, and remember, when they brought her to her grave, they carried her upside-down. They buried her facedown, as they do all witches. All those they are afraid to burn.'

Adam was confused. 'What does that mean?' he asked.

Bum would tell them no more. He shook his head and returned to feeding the birds.

'It's a riddle,' he said. 'You figure it out.'

Six

'Well, that's just great,' Sally said a few minutes later as they walked back up the hill in the direction of Adam's house. 'He gets us all excited about hearing the big secret, and then he just tells us a stupid riddle.'

'You were excited?' Adam asked. 'I thought you didn't want to find the Secret Path.'

'I'm human,' Sally said. 'I can change my mind.' She glanced over at Watch, who had been silent since Bum had sent them on their way. 'Aren't you disappointed?'

'Not yet,' Watch said.

Sally stopped him. 'You're not trying to figure out the riddle, are you?'

Watch shrugged. 'Of course.'

'But it's meaningless,' Sally said. 'How can we follow the life of the witch who founded this town? She's been dead almost two hundred years. And what does it mean anyway? A life isn't a line on the ground. You can't follow it as you would a path.'

'That part of the riddle is easy,' Watch said. He glanced at Adam. 'Have you figured it out?'

Adam had struggled with the riddle since Bum had told them. But he had been hesitant to say anything because he feared he might make a fool of himself. Watch was obviously the most intelligent one in the group. He spoke quietly as he answered Watch's question.

'I was thinking to follow her life meant to follow where she went during her life,' Adam said.

'That's ridiculous,' Sally said.

'It's probably true,' Watch said. 'It's the only explanation. What puzzles me is what's so special about each place she went.'

'Maybe the places aren't so important as the order they're in,' Adam said. 'Maybe the Secret Path is right in front of us, like the numbers on a combination lock. But you have to turn the numbers in the exact right way. And only then will the lock open.'

Sally stared at them, dumbfounded. 'I can't believe you guys. You both think you're Sherlock Holmes. Bum's just taking you for a ride. He only wants you to bring him another sandwich, and then he'll tell you another stupid riddle. He'll keep going until you've fed him the entire summer.'

Watch ignored her. 'I think you're right, Adam,' he said, impressed. 'The path must be right in front of us. It's the sequence that's important – where you go first, second, third. Let's try to figure out the first place. Where was Madeline Templeton born?'

'I don't know,' Adam said. 'I never heard of the woman until this morning.'

Watch turned to Sally. 'Do you know where she was born?'

Sally continued to pout. 'I think this is stupid.' She paused. 'At the beach.'

'How do you know?' Watch asked, surprised.

'There's the old story about how Madeline Templeton was brought to earth by a flock of seagulls on a dark and stormy night,' Sally explained. 'In fact, she was supposed to have come out of the sky exactly where we just were with Bum.' Sally made a face. 'If you can believe that.'

'You believe everything else,' Adam said.

'I draw the line at supernatural births,' Sally replied.

'The story may have a germ of truth in it,' Watch said. 'As long as the location of her birth is correct, it doesn't matter if birds, or her mother, brought her into the world. And if the location is accurate, we don't have to search for the first place on the Secret Path – we've already been there.' He considered for a moment. 'It makes sense to me. Bum insisted on telling me the riddle at that exact spot. Maybe he knew we would have trouble finding the first location.'

'Where did she go next?' Adam asked. 'How can we know?'

'We may not have to know every detail of what she did,' Watch said. 'We can just follow the general direction of her life. There are so many stories about Madeline Templeton that this won't be as hard as it sounds. For example, I know that when she was five she was supposed to have wandered into the Derby Tree and made all the leaves turn red.'

'How could a kid get inside a tree?' Adam asked.

'She was no ordinary kid,' Sally explained. 'And it's no ordinary tree. It's still alive, up on Derby Street, an old oak with branches shaped like clawed hands. Its leaves are always red, year-round. They look like they were dipped in blood. And there's a large hole in it. You can actually slide inside and sit down, one person at a time. But if you do, your brains get scrambled.'

'I've been in it,' Watch said. 'My brain didn't get scrambled.'

'Are you sure?' Sally asked.

'After that what did she do?' Adam asked.

Watch started walking back up the hill. 'Let's talk about that on the way to the tree. I think I have an idea.'

Seven

The tree was as weird as Sally had described. Standing alone in the centre of an open space, it looked as if it had witnessed many bloody battles and been splattered in the process. The branches hung low to the ground, ready to swoop up any kid who ran by. Adam spotted the large hole in the side. It looked like a hungry maw. The edges were rough – sharp teeth waiting to come together.

'I know a kid who went in there and came out speaking in tongues,' Sally said. 'Snake tongues.'

'It's just a tree that's been cursed,' Watch said. 'I'll go in first to show you there's no danger.'

'How can we believe you when you come out?' Sally asked. 'You might not even be human.'

'Oh, brother,' Adam said, although he was glad Watch was going first. There was something pretty scary about a tree with blood-red leaves at the beginning of summer.

Together, Sally and Adam watched as Watch walked over to the tree and climbed inside the hole. A minute went by and Watch didn't reappear.

'What's taking him so long?' Adam wondered aloud.

'The tree is probably digesting him,' Sally said.

'How did it get the name the Derby Tree?' Adam asked.

'Old man Derby tried to chop it down once,' Sally explained. 'I was only five years old at the time, but I remember the day. He blamed the tree for the disappearance of one of his kids. He had like ten of them, so he could stand to lose one. Anyway, he came here one morning with a huge axe and took a swing at the tree. He missed and accidentally cut off one of his legs. You'll see Derby walking around town on a wooden leg. All the kids call him Mr Stilts. He'd be the first to tell you that tree is evil.'

'I just wish Watch would get back out here,' Adam said. He cupped his hands round his mouth and called out, 'Watch!'

Watch didn't answer. Another five minutes went by. Adam was on the verge of running for help when their friend finally poked his head out. He squeezed through the hole with difficulty. It was as if the opening had shrunk since he'd been inside. He walked over to them like nothing had happened.

'Why were you inside so long?' Sally demanded.

'What are you talking about?' Watch asked, checking one of his many watches. 'I just went inside for a second.'

'You were in there at least an hour,' Sally said.

'It was closer to ten minutes,' Adam corrected.

Watch scratched his thinning blond hair. 'That's weird – it didn't feel that long.'

'Didn't you hear us calling for you?' Sally asked.

'No,' Watch said. 'Inside the tree you can't hear a thing.' He paused. 'Who wants to go next?'

'I will,' Adam said, anxious to get it over.

'Wait a second,' Sally said to Watch. 'How do we know you haven't been altered in some way?'

'I'm fine,' Watch said.

'You wouldn't know if you're fine if you've been changed,' Sally said. 'You'd be the last person to know. Let me ask you a couple of questions just to be sure your brain hasn't been operated on. Who's the most beautiful girl in Spooksville?'

'You are,' Watch said.

'And who's the best poet in Spooksville?' Sally asked.

'You are,' Watch said.

'You write poetry?' Adam asked her.

'Yes, and they're awful poems,' Sally said. 'I think he's been altered.'

45

'If I have, it happened a long time ago,' Watch said. 'Give it a try, Adam. I want to move on to the next spot.'

'All right,' Adam said, feeling far from excited about the prospect. He walked slowly towards the tree and, as he did, a breeze stirred the red leaves, making it look as if they were excited about him coming close. Adam's heart thumped in his chest. Obviously time moved at a different pace inside the tree. Maybe when he emerged Sally and Watch would be old, like his parents. Maybe he'd get out, but become a part of the tree, a sad face cut into its thick bark.

The hole definitely seemed smaller than it had ten minutes earlier, maybe half the size it had been. Adam realised he had to get in and out quickly. Still, he hesitated. A strange odour spilled out from the interior of the tree. It could have been the smell of blood. Plus, as he stood under the tree, he couldn't help noticing how far away his friends appeared to be. They were where he'd left them, but they could have been a mile away. He waved to them and it was several seconds before they waved back. Weird.

'I have to do it,' Adam whispered to himself. 'If I don't, Sally will know I'm a coward.'

Summoning his courage, Adam ducked his head and squirmed through the hole into the tree. He was able to get his whole body inside, and turn round, although he had to keep his head down. Standing hunched over, he peered through the hole and was surprised to see that everything outside had lost its colour. It was as if he were looking at a black-and-white film. Also, as Watch had said, the interior of the tree was completely silent. All Adam could hear was his panting and the pounding of his heart. It seemed to him that the tree was also listening to his heart, wondering how much blood it pumped a day. How much blood the reckless boy had to feed its hungry branches . . .

'I got to get out of here,' Adam said to himself. He tried to squeeze back out. Now there was no doubt, the entrance had shrunk. Adam got halfway out and then felt his midsection catch. Sucking in a strangled breath, he tried to let out a scream, but failed. The bark had him in a vice-like grip! And the way it was closing on him, he would be cut in half!

'Help!' he managed to get out. Sally and Watch were at his side in a moment. Watch yanked at his arms. Sally pulled at his hair. But he stayed stuck. The pain in his sides was incredible – he felt like his guts were about to explode. 'Oh,' he moaned.

Sally was near hysterics as she pulled his hair out by the roots. 'Do something, Watch!' she screamed. 'It's eating his legs.'

'It's not eating my legs,' Adam complained. 'It's breaking me in two.'

'A dying man shouldn't quibble,' Sally said. 'Watch!'

'I know what to do,' Watch said, letting go of Adam's arms. He pulled out a Bic lighter and ran over to a drooping branch. As Adam struggled to draw in a breath, Watch flicked the Bic and held the flame under a particularly big and ugly branch. The tree reacted as if it had been stung. The branch snapped back, the leaves almost slapping Watch. At that exact moment Adam felt the grip on him lessen.

'Pull me now!' he shouted to the others.

Watch returned to Adam's side and, with Sally's help, yanked Adam free. Adam landed face first on the rough ground and scratched his cheeks. But the slight injury was overshadowed by his immense relief. He drew in a deep, shuddering breath and tried to crawl further away from the tree. Sally and Watch helped him to his feet. Behind them, Adam noticed that the hole had all but vanished.

'You can see why old man Derby wanted to chop it down,' Sally panted.

'Yeah,' Adam gasped, gently probing his sides for broken ribs. He seemed to be in one piece, although he knew he'd be sore the next day. If he lived that long. Suddenly he had lost all enthusiasm for finding the rest of the Secret

Path. 'There's no way you're going in there,' he told Sally.

'I don't know if climbing inside the tree is a requirement,' Watch said. 'It's probably good enough that we came here.'

'Now you tell me,' Adam said.

'Let's quit while we're ahead,' Sally said. 'This path is too dangerous.'

'Let's go a little further,' Watch said. 'I know what's next. It can't be that dangerous.' He paused to look back at the tree. 'I hope.'

Eight

There were other interesting stories surrounding Madeline Templeton. Watch related several of them while they hiked toward their next destination. When she was sixteen, she was supposed to have climbed up to one of the largest of the caves that overlooked Spooksville and wrestled a huge mountain lion.

'She supposedly killed the lion with her nails,' Watch said. 'She wore them long.'

'I heard the tips of them were poisonous,' Sally added.

'Are we going to this cave next?' Adam asked unenthusiastically. He was scared of entering any more places that could abruptly close round him.

'Yes,' Watch said. 'I've been there before and had no problems.'

'You were inside the tree before, too, and had no problems,' Sally reminded him.

'We'll go in together,' Watch said. 'We should be safe.'

'Sounds like a plan for disaster,' Sally remarked. 'But assuming we survive the cave, have you figured out the rest of the path? I don't want to waste all my time and energy hiking in circles round this city I hate.'

Watch nodded. 'I think I've remembered the highlights of her life. We hit the cave next, then head for the chapel.'

'Why the chapel?' Sally asked. 'I don't think it existed when Madeline was alive.'

'It didn't,' Watch said. 'But she got married on the spot where the chapel was later built. She was twenty-eight years old. That would be the next big event in her life that we know about. After the chapel, I think we have to visit the reservoir.'

'What happened at the reservoir?' Adam asked.

'That's where she drowned her husband,' Sally said.

'That's what the stories say,' Watch added. 'People say she tied his legs down with heavy stones and pushed him screaming off a boat that was floating in the centre of the reservoir.'

'Why?' Adam asked.

'She thought he was chasing another woman,' Sally said. 'Turned out she was wrong. But she didn't find out until after she buried the other woman alive.'

'Wonderful,' Adam said.

'After the reservoir, we go back to the beach,' Watch said. 'That's where the townsfolk tried to burn her alive for being a witch – the first time.'

'What do you mean they *tried* to burn her?' Adam asked.

'The wood they stacked up round her refused to catch fire,' Sally said. 'And snakes crawled out of it and killed the judge who condemned her to death. You remember that story the next time you get the urge to visit her great-great-great-great-granddaughter, Ann Templeton.'

'After the beach, we go to the cemetery,' Watch said.

Sally stopped him in midstride. 'There's no way we're going there. Even you know that's a stupid idea. Dead people live there. Live people die there.'

'She was buried in the cemetery,' Watch said. 'To reach the end of the Secret Path, we must follow her life to the end. Bum made that clear.'

'Bum was anything but clear,' Sally said.

'Let's worry about the cemetery when we get that far,' Watch said.

'Yeah,' Sally said sarcastically. 'We might be ready for the cemetery by then. We might be dead.'

They hiked up to one of the largest caves that overlooked Spooksville. Adam was breathing hard by the time they reached it, and was getting hungry. From the outside cave didn't appear threatening. The opening was wide;

none of them would have to squeeze inside. But the moment they stepped inside, Adam felt the temperature drop at least ten degrees. He asked Watch about it.

'Underground streams flow beneath these caves,' Watch said. 'The water in them is freezing. If you listen closely you can hear the splashing.'

Adam stopped and listened. Not only did he hear a faint splashing sound, but an even fainter moaning sound. 'What's that?' he asked the others.

'Ghosts,' Sally said.

'There are no ghosts,' Adam said indignantly.

'Listen to Mr Realist,' Sally mocked. 'He doesn't believe in ghosts even though a tree almost ate him an hour ago.' She turned to Watch. 'We've done our duty – we came here. We don't have to stay. Let's go.'

Watch agreed. They left the cave without being attacked and hiked toward the chapel. Sally wanted to visit the reservoir first, since it was along the way. But Watch insisted they stick to the correct sequence.

The chapel turned out to be the least scary place, although the church bell began to ring as they walked up, and didn't stop until they walked away. Sally thought the bell was trying to warn them to turn back.

'Before it's too late,' she said.

The reservoir was creepy, the water an odd colour, sort

of greyish. Adam was unhappy to learn that all the town water came from it. The area around it was similar to the space inside the tree; it was unnaturally silent. Their words, as they spoke, seemed to die in the air. Sally wondered out loud how many bodies were buried under the water's surface.

'I don't know,' Watch said. 'But I do know that no fish can live in this reservoir.'

'They die?' Adam asked.

'Yes,' Watch said. 'They throw themselves on to the shore and die.'

'They would rather die than live here,' Sally said.

'Kansas City didn't have these kind of problems,' Adam said.

They returned to the beach. By this time the day was wearing on, and Adam thought his parents would be worrying about him. But Watch was against his going home and telling them he was OK.

'We don't want to wander off the path,' Watch said. 'We might have to start over at the beginning.'

'You might also be about to disappear permanently,' Sally said. 'It's better you don't give your parents any false reassurances.'

Bum was no longer at the beach, and Watch wasn't sure where the angry crowd had tried to burn Madeline

Templeton two hundred years ago. But Watch suspected they'd tried to kill her near the jetty because that's where the wood from the ocean usually washed up on shore.

'They were lazy in those days,' Watch said. 'When they wanted to burn someone to death, they didn't like to search for wood.'

The jetty felt sufficiently creepy, but Adam was too distracted by the thought of the cemetery that was to come next to worry about it. Ordinary cemeteries were not on Adam's list of favourite places to visit, and he suspected Spooksville's cemetery would be a hundred times worse than a normal one. As they walked toward it, Sally didn't exactly try to put his mind at ease.

'A lot of the people buried in Spooksville aren't completely dead,' she said. 'The local undertaker is always out hustling business. If you have a bad cold, he wants you to come down to his showroom to pick out a coffin, just in case the cold goes into your chest and you choke to death. I've got to admit, though, a tour of his stock can make you get better in a hurry.'

'I don't believe any undertaker could be so crude and cruel,' Adam said.

'I've heard scratching sounds coming from underground while walking in the cemetery,' Watch said. 'I think a few people got boxed up a little too soon.'

56

'That's horrible,' Adam said, appalled. 'Why didn't you get a shovel and dig those people out?'

'I have a bad back,' Watch said.

'And you don't want to go digging up people who've been in the ground for a few days,' Sally said. 'They might try to eat your brains.'

Adam began to have second thoughts. 'I've had kind of a long day, moving and getting attacked by the tree and all. Maybe I should catch up with you guys later.'

'Are you chickening out?' Sally asked.

'No,' Adam said quickly. 'I'm just stating a fact.' He paused. 'Besides, you've been against this quest from the start.'

'It's my nature to be against anything unnatural,' Sally said. 'And I think this Secret Path qualifies.'

'If you really are scared,' Watch said, 'I don't want to force you into it, Adam.'

'I told you guys, I'm not scared,' Adam said quickly. 'I'm just tired.'

'No problem,' Watch said.

'We won't hold your sudden and unexpected wave of tiredness against you,' Sally added.

'It's not sudden and unexpected,' Adam protested. 'If you'd just moved here from Kansas City, you'd be tired, too.'

'Particularly if I was about to visit a cemetery where people are often buried alive,' Sally said.

'I told you, I don't believe in ghosts,' Adam said. 'They don't scare me.'

'Good for you,' Sally said.

Adam felt cornered and humiliated. 'All right, all right. I'll go to the cemetery. But that's as far as I'll go. I have to get home right after.'

'If what Bum said is true,' Watch warned, 'you might not get home until very late.'

Nine

The cemetery was surrounded by a high grey brick wall. The front gate was made of wrought iron; rusted metal bars twisted upward into point shapes. The few trees that littered the grave site were limp and colourless; they looked like the skeletons of real trees. Adam could see no way in and felt a moment of relief. They'd have to quit. Unfortunately, Watch had other ideas.

'There're some loose bricks round the back,' Watch said. 'If you suck in your breath, you can just squeeze through the space.'

'What if we get stuck?' Adam asked.

'You of all people should know the answer to that question,' Sally said.

'The brick wall won't hurt you,' Watch said. 'It isn't alive.'

'Just like the people locked inside,' Sally said menacingly.

Getting through the small opening proved easy. But once they were inside and making their way round the tombstones, Adam began to get the sinking feeling that nothing else would be easy. He definitely didn't want to be fooling around the dead witch's grave. He could see her old castle peering down at them; a tall tower rose from the rear of the huge stone building. He thought he caught sight of a dull red light glowing from a window at the highest point. The light of a fire perhaps, of many candles at least. He could imagine Ann Templeton sitting in that tower in a black robe and staring into a crystal ball. Watching the three kids who dared to defile her ancestor's grave. Cursing them for even thinking about it. She was a beautiful woman, true, but striding toward her great-great-great-great-grandmother's grave, Adam began to believe Sally's warnings about Ann.

He began to believe that Spooksville really did deserve its wicked name.

Madeline Templeton's tombstone was larger than any other in the cemetery. Its shape was odd. Rather than having a cross at the top, or a half dome, the top of the dark marble was cut in the shape of a raven. The bird glared down at them as if they were its prey, ready to pounce. Adam blinked up at the deep black eyes that seemed to stare back at him. Over and around the grave, on all sides, the ground was bare. Adam realised that no grass could grow so close to the remains of a witch.

'What a nice place for a picnic,' Sally said sarcastically. She turned to Watch. 'What do we do now? Wish ourselves into another dimension?'

'I don't think it's that easy,' Watch said. 'We have to figure out the last part of the riddle.' He paused and repeated Bum's words: ' "Follow her all the way to her death, and remember, when they brought her to her grave, they carried her upside-down. They buried her facedown, as they do all witches. All those they are afraid to burn." ' Watch paused to clean his glasses on his shirt. 'I don't think any of us can walk in here upside-down.'

'That's a pity,' Adam said.

'You look heartbroken, Adam,' Sally said.

Watch began to walk round the large tombstone. He gestured in the direction of the cemetery's entrance. 'That must have been the entrance even then, so they must have carried her coffin in from over there. We should probably start there and walk this way. But I don't think that's going to work. Bum was trying to tell us something more with his riddle.' Watch frowned. 'Do either of you have any ideas?'

'Not me,' Sally said, pacing several steps away from the grave and plopping down on the ground. 'I'm too tired, too hungry.' She patted the spot beside her. 'Why don't you rest, Adam?'

'I think we've done pretty well to figure out any of the riddle,' Adam said, joining Sally on the ground. It was good to rest; he felt as if he'd just walked to the West Coast from Kansas City. He called over to Watch, who continued to stroll around the tombstone, 'We can always decipher the last part later.'

Sally smiled at Adam. 'Do you want me to rub your feet?' she asked sweetly.

'That's all right,' Adam said.

'I have a gentle touch,' Sally said.

'Save your strength,' Adam said.

'We could get a coffin,' Watch suggested from behind the tombstone. 'And I could lie inside it upside-down and the two of you could carry me over here.'

'The coffins they sell in town lock when you close them,' Sally said, lying back and staring up at the sky. 'Remember the scratching sounds.'

'I don't think we have the strength to carry you in a coffin,' Adam said, distracted as he watched the dull red light radiating from the top of the nearby castle tower begin to flicker. Actually, it wasn't so dull any more. Maybe Ann Templeton had decided to light more candles or throw another log on the fire. What did she do up there? Adam wondered. Was she really a witch? Could she really turn boys into frogs and girls into lizards? Adam couldn't get her voice out of his head. While Watch continued to poke around behind him, and Sally lay snoozing, Adam thought of the strange things she had said to him.

'*Nothing is the way it looks. Nobody is just one way. When you hear stories about me – perhaps from this skinny girl here, perhaps from others – know that they're only partially true.*'

But she had seemed to like him.

'*You have such nice eyes, did you know that, Adam?*'

Adam didn't think she'd try to hurt him.

'*I will see both of you later – under different circumstances.*'

The light in the tall tower flared again.

Candles didn't usually burn so red.

Adam found himself unable to quit staring at the light.

At the tower.

He thought he saw the shadow of Ann Templeton step to the window.

'*Would you like to visit me there someday?*'

Ann looked down at him. Smiled down at him.

Her lips the colour of fire. Her eyes glowing like a cat's.

'Oh, no,' Adam whispered to himself.

Sally nudged him in the side.

'Adam?' she said, sounding worried.

'Yes,' he mumbled, feeling hypnotised.

Sally shook him. 'Adam!'

He looked over at her. 'What's the matter?' he said.

'What's the matter with you?' Sally looked up at the castle tower. 'She's trying to put a spell on you.'

Adam shook himself. The red light was gone, the image of the beautiful woman – as if the structure had been deserted for two hundred years. 'No. I'm fine, really.' He did feel kind of cold, though. 'But I think we should get out of here.' He glanced round. 'Where's Watch?'

Sally frowned. 'I don't know.' She jumped to her feet. 'Watch! Watch! Adam, I don't see him! Watch!'

They called for ten minutes without stopping.

But their friend was gone.

Ten

They found Watch's glasses in the dirt in front of the tombstone. Adam half expected to discover a bloodstain on them when he picked them up. But they were only dirty.

'Watch can't walk ten feet without his glasses,' Sally whispered.

'But he must have walked out of here,' Adam said.

'No,' Sally replied gloomily.

'What are you saying? He's gone.'

'But he didn't walk out of here. He vanished.'

'I didn't see him vanish,' Adam said.

'What did you see?'

Adam was confused. 'I don't know. I was staring up at that tower.' He pointed through the skeleton trees toward Ann Templeton's home. 'There was a red glow coming from the highest window.' He shook his head and peered up at the sky. 'It seems later than it should be. Did we fall asleep?'

Sally, also, appeared puzzled. 'I didn't think so. I know I just lay down for a minute. But then – I think I dreamed.'

'What did you dream?' Adam asked.

Fear entered Sally's eyes. 'About the day they buried the witch. I saw them carry her body in here. They were all scared. They thought it might come back to life and eat them.' She shook her head. 'But it was just a dream.'

Adam gestured with Watch's glasses in his hand. 'We have to find Watch.' He turned towards the back of the cemetery, where they'd entered. Sally stopped him.

'Watch didn't leave the cemetery,' she said firmly.

'Then where is he?' Adam asked.

'Don't you see? He found the end of the Secret Path.' She pointed at the witch's tombstone. 'He went through there.'

Adam shook his head. 'That's impossible. Why would he be the only one to vanish? Why not us?'

'He did something – special. You're sure you didn't see him?'

'I told you, I didn't.'

Sally walked round the tombstone, talking all the time. 'He was trying to figure out what the end of Bum's riddle meant. He must have hit upon the solution, maybe even by accident.' She paused to consider, reciting the lines once more. ' "Follow her all the way to her death, and remember, when they brought her to her grave, they carried her upside-down." ' Sally shook her head. 'Watch couldn't have walked up to the tombstone upside-down. There was no one to carry him.'

Adam had an idea. 'Maybe we're looking at the riddle too literally. It is a riddle, after all. "Upside-down" is another way of saying "backward".'

Sally came closer. 'I don't understand.'

Adam pointed toward the cemetery entrance. 'Bum might have been telling us she was brought in here backwards. Maybe all we have to do, here at the end of the Secret Path, is approach the tombstone walking backward.'

Sally jumped. 'Let's try it!'

'Wait a second. What if it works?'

'We want it to work. We have to give Watch his glasses.' Sally paused. 'You're not getting scared again?'

Adam spoke impatiently. 'I wasn't scared to begin with. What I'm saying is even if we do go through the doorway into another dimension, how do we know we'll end up in the same dimension Watch is in? Bum said there were many Spooksvilles on the other side.'

'I guess there's no way of telling unless we try. We'll just have to risk it.'

Adam shook his head. 'I'll risk it. Alone. You stay here and stand guard.'

'What am I standing guard against? All the danger's on the other side. I'm coming with you.'

'No. You said it yourself – it could be dangerous.'

Sally stared at him. 'You're not just trying to impress me, are you? Because if you are, it's not necessary. I like you already.'

Adam sighed. 'I'm not trying to impress. I'm just trying to keep you from getting killed.'

Sally snorted. 'Adam, you just got here. I grew up in Spooksville. Dark doorways are an everyday occurrence for me.' She reached for his hand. 'Come, we'll go together, holding on to each other. That way if we end up in the witch's evil realm, I'll have someone cute to keep me company for the rest of eternity.'

Adam hesitated. 'You really think I'm cute?'

'Yes. But don't let it go to your head.' She paused. 'Don't you think I'm cute?'

Adam shrugged. 'Well, yes, I suppose. You look all right.'

Sally socked him. 'All right? I look all right? Brother, you have a thing or two to learn about insecure females.' She took his hand. 'Let's do this quick before I lose my nerve.'

Adam could feel her trembling. 'You are scared, aren't you?'

Sally nodded. 'I'm terrified.'

Adam nodded. 'So am I.' He tightened his grip on Watch's glasses. 'But we've got to try. Our friend could be in danger.'

'You sound like a hero on a movie of the week,' Sally said.

'I've been called worse.'

Together they walked to the entrance of the cemetery. Then, still holding hands, they began to walk backwards toward the tombstone. It was difficult because they had to keep glancing over their shoulders to keep from stumbling. Adam found, as they neared the grave, that his heart was pounding wildly. The sky seemed to dim. Out of the corner of his eye, he thought he saw a red light flicker in the tower of Ann Templeton's castle. He believed he saw her image beckoning him. Laughing at him.

The tombstone rose up behind them.

The wind stirred. Dust flew. Blinding them.

'Adam!' Sally cried suddenly.

Adam felt himself stumble. No, it was more as if he'd tripped and fallen off a cliff. An invisible precipice at the edge of the world. The earth disappeared beneath his feet; the sky ceased to exist. He fell without moving. He continued to grip Sally's hand, although she could have been a million light-years away for all he could see of her. In fact, he could see nothing, not even the dark storm that lifted him up as swiftly as it threw him down. Dropping him in another time, in another dimension.

Eleven

The tombstone stood before them. In a dark and dreary new place.

'We've been turned round,' Sally whispered, standing beside Adam, still holding his hand.

'We've been more than turned round,' Adam whispered back.

He was right – boy, was he right. The sky was not completely dark, but washed by a faint red glow. It was as if the haunting light of Ann Templeton's tower had spread from horizon to horizon. The trees were now totally bare, sharp sticks waiting to scratch whoever walked by. All round them the tombstones were toppled and broken, covered with cobwebs and dust. Many had fallen, it seemed, because the bodies they marked had dug themselves out from under the ground. Adam shuddered as he saw how many broken and splintered coffins were scattered about the cemetery.

In the distance, in the direction of the castle, they heard screams, the cries of the doomed.

'We have to get out of here!' Sally cried. 'Let's go back through the tombstone.'

'What about Watch?' Adam asked.

'If he's here, it's probably too late for him.' They heard another scream and Sally jerked Adam's hand. 'Quick, let's go! Before something dead eats us!'

Once more they approached the tombstone walking backwards. But this time they just bumped up against the marble. It was solid, no longer a portal into another dimension. They were trapped.

'What's wrong?' Sally cried.

'It's not working,' Adam said.

'I know that, but why isn't it working?'

'I don't know. I just got here from Kansas City, remember.' Another cry sounded from the direction of the castle. Off to their left, in the corner of the cemetery, something stirred beneath the ground, scattering dirt and dead leaves. It could have been another corpse clawing its way to the surface. They didn't wait to find out.

'Let's get out of here!' Sally cried.

They ran for the entrance, which was now only a heap of rusted metal. Exiting the cemetery, they caught sight of the sea, far below. Only it no longer looked as if it were filled with water. The ocean glowed an eerie green, like liquid that had gushed from radioactive mines. A mysterious fog hung over it, whirling in tiny cyclones. Even from a distance Adam believed he saw shapes moving beneath the surface. Hungry aquatic creatures. He and Sally paused to catch their breaths.

'This is worse than *The Twilight Zone*,' he muttered.

'I want to go to my house,' Sally said.

'Do we really want to go there?' Adam wondered aloud. 'What will we find?'

Sally nodded in understanding. 'Maybe we'll find this creepy dimension's counterpart of ourselves.'

It was a terrifying idea. 'Do you think it's possible?'

'I think anything is possible here,' Sally said grimly. Another scream echoed from the direction of the castle. It sounded as if some poor soul had just been dropped in a vat of boiling water. Sally squeezed Adam's hand and continued, 'But I would rather be here than there.'

'I agree,' Adam said.

So they headed for their houses, but it was like no walk through the gentle streets of the *real* Spooksville. In fact, they didn't even walk on the pavement. Instead, they darted from bush to bush, tree to tree, in case they'd be seen. Yet they saw no one, at least not clearly. But round every corner they thought they caught a glimpse of someone fleeing, or else the shadow of something fleeing or following them.

'This place looks as if it's been through a war,' Sally whispered.

Adam nodded. 'A war with the forces of evil.'

The houses were in ruins. Many had been burned to the ground. Smoke drifted up from the ashes, mingling with the fog that was moving in from the direction of the glowing green sea. Most of the houses, like the tombstones in the cemetery, were covered with dust and cobwebs.

What had driven the people away? Adam wondered. What had taken the place of the people? Black shapes moved against the dull red sky, bats the size of horses screeched wickedly as they wheeled in search of living food. Holding on to each other, Sally and Adam hurried home.

They went to Sally's house first, which may have been a mistake. It was scarcely there. A large tree that she said didn't even exist in the real world had fallen across the roof and crushed the house flat. Searching through the ruins, they couldn't find any sign of her parents.

'Maybe they got away,' she said.

'Maybe you wouldn't have even recognised them,' Adam said.

Sally shivered. 'Do you still want to go to your house?'

'I don't know what else to do. We may be trapped here for ever.'

'Don't say that.'

'It's true.'

Sally was gloomy. 'A lot of sad things are true.'

Twelve

Adam's house was still standing. He knocked on the door before entering. No one answered. Fog crept round them, glowing reddish orange like the sky. In this place Halloween could be a year-round holiday. Adam put his ear to the door, listening for talking vampires, for zombies walking.

'We don't have to go inside,' Sally said.

Adam frowned. 'I have to see how they are.'

'*They* might be more like *things*.'

Adam reached for the doorknob. 'You can stay here if you want.'

Sally glanced round from the dusty porch. 'Why didn't you convince me to stay on the other side of the tombstone?'

'I tried.'

'I remember.' Sally nodded. 'Let's do it.'

Inside it was dark. Big surprise. The lights didn't work. They moved through the living-room to the kitchen. A roast turkey was set out on the table. The only trouble was a bunch of maggots and worms had got to it. The insects were crawling in and out of the dark meat and the white meat. Adam tried the tap – he was thirsty. Steam bubbled out into the filthy sink.

'Cheery,' Sally said.

They went upstairs to the bedrooms. Adam peeked inside his first, holding his breath, waiting for a claw to reach out from the wardrobe and rip open his face. But there was no one there. Only dusty books that he had bought years ago, in the real world. A favourite coat a friend had given him in Kansas City was held suspended in midair by a gigantic cobweb.

'It's over there,' Sally whispered, pointing to the corner.

The black spider was the size of a cat and covered with hair that stood up like greasy spikes. It glanced over at them as they peered through the door and clicked its bloodstained fangs. They quickly shut the door.

'I don't suppose we could call for an exterminator in this place,' Sally muttered.

Adam peered into his sister's room next. It was also empty, except for another giant spider. But in his parents' bedroom, on the bed, he saw two shapes lying under the dirty sheet. With Sally grimacing at his back, he approached the bed slowly.

'Maybe we shouldn't disturb the shapes,' she whispered, tense.

'I have to see,' Adam said softly.

'No,' Sally implored, grabbing the back of his shirt. Adam almost jumped out of his skin.

'Don't do that!' he hissed.

'I hear something outside. Coming this way.'

Adam paused. He heard nothing. 'It's just your imagination.'

'My *imagination*? I don't need an imagination in this place.' She glanced towards the two forms beneath the sheets. 'Come on, you don't want to look.'

Adam shook her off. 'I have to.'

He stepped forward and reached over. He slowly removed the sheet.

He gasped.

They'd been dead a long time. This man and woman skeleton. Ants the size of beetles crawled over their bony arms. Their hair hung over their dry skulls like dried-out straw soaked in rust. Their jawbones hung open. Adam quickly replaced the sheet as tears filled his eyes.

'That's not my mother and father,' he said, sobbing.

Sally put a gentle hand on his shoulder. 'Of course not. Your parents are alive in the real world. When we get back to them, you'll see that. It will be like waking from a bad dream.'

Adam shook his head. 'This is no dream.'

Sally suddenly froze. 'Something is coming this way!'

Adam heard it now. It sounded like the beating of a horse's hooves.

'It is coming this way,' he whispered.

'We have to hide,' Sally said, getting frantic. 'It's coming for us.' She pulled on his arm. 'We have to get out of here!'

Adam grabbed her. 'Wait! This is as good a hiding-place as any. Let's stay here.'

She pointed to the bed. 'With them?'

Adam cautioned her to speak softly. 'We'll just wait until the hooves pass.'

But the sound did not pass. Instead it stopped directly outside the house. 'Now we're in trouble,' Sally moaned.

They heard footsteps, the pounding of a human in boots on the path. Whoever it was reached the door and, without pausing, kicked it in. The sound of the splintering wood made Adam's heart skip. Grabbing Sally, he pulled her out of the room and down the hallway. He barely knew the layout of the house, having just moved in – in that other dimension. But he did remember there was a window beside the hall cupboard, one that led out on to the roof.

From there it was a quick hop into the garden.

Adam got to the window just as the thundering steps reached the top of the stairs.

At the far end of the hallway he saw a tall figure clad in chain mail turn their way.

It looked like a knight. A black knight.

In its right hand it carried a long silver sword.

It didn't look friendly.

Adam yanked the window open and pushed Sally head first through it and on to the broken wooden roof shingles. As she groped over the slippery roof, Adam tried to squirm out of the window, too. But the knight, although fitted with heavy armour from head to toe, was quick on his feet. Before Adam could get all the way out of the window, something hard and heavy knocked his legs out from under him. Toppling back inside the house, he caught a glimpse of the knight raising the sharp silver sword.

Adam felt sure he was about to have his head cut from his body.

There was a flash of light and everything went black.

Thirteen

When Adam awoke, he felt cold and sore. Opening his eyes, he found himself in a stone dungeon. He heard someone breathing beside him and rolled over on his back. He squinted in the poor light.

'Who's there?' he whispered.

'Watch. Is that you, Adam?'

Adam felt a wave of relief. Until he realised his hand was bolted to the wall with a steel wristband. As his eyes adjusted to the dark, he saw that they were ringed in by metal bars, trapped tight in a tiny prison.

'Yeah, it's me,' Adam replied. 'Where are we?'

'In the basement of the witch's castle,' Watch said, moving closer. He, too, was bolted to the stone wall, but he had enough slack to manoeuvre so he could actually reach out and touch Adam. His eyes blinked as he stared at him. 'You wouldn't by any chance have my glasses, would you?' Watch asked.

Adam felt in his pocket. 'As a matter of fact, I do,' he replied. He handed the glasses to Watch, who had to bend them to fit his face. Adam figured he must have crushed them when he was knocked out. He checked his head for injuries, glad it was still attached to his neck. He had a large bump on the top of his skull but otherwise seemed OK. His back and legs, however, were cold and stiff from having lain on the hard stone floor. 'How long have I been out?' he asked.

'They brought you in two hours ago,' Watch said, still adjusting his glasses.

'What about Sally?' Adam asked.

'Did she come through to this dimension?'

'Yes. I tried to stop her. Have you seen her?'

'No,' Watch said. 'But that might be good.'

'Why?'

'I think the witch has an unpleasant surprise in store for us.'

'Have you seen her?' Adam asked. 'What does she look like?'

With his free hand, Watch scratched his head in the dark. 'She looks like Ann Templeton, but with red hair instead of black. But for all I know Ann Templeton looks just the same as Madeline Templeton did.'

'You mean, the witch who died two hundred years ago might be holding us captive?'

'Yeah. Or else Ann Templeton's counterpart in this dimension is keeping us prisoner. It's hard to tell which.'

Once more, Adam remembered Ann Templeton's words to him.

'*I will see both of you later, under different circumstances.*'

'I think it's probably Ann Templeton's counterpart,' Adam said, thoughtful. 'I hope it is. She didn't seem that mean.'

'You haven't met her,' Watch said. 'I have. She sends her black knight out to collect boys and girls. I've seen some of the kids who've been here a while. They're all missing at least one body part – either a nose, or eyes, or ears. Or even a mouth.'

'*You have such nice eyes, did you know that, Adam?*'

Adam was horrified. 'What does she do with these – parts?'

Watch shrugged. 'Maybe she just collects them, the way I collect stamps.'

'You collect stamps? I collect baseball cards.' Adam shook his head. 'I don't suppose she'd want to trade our collections for our freedom.' He paused. 'How did you get here? Did the black knight grab you?'

'Yeah. He got me as soon as I came through to this side. He was waiting for me in the cemetery.'

'Then he must have known you were coming,' Adam said.

Watch was thoughtful. 'I was thinking that myself. That means Ann Templeton must have been watching us from her castle and realised what we were doing. She must have been able to communicate that information to the witch on this side.' Watch shook his head. 'But I don't see how we can use that fact to escape.'

'Were you awake when they brought you in here?' Adam asked.

'Yeah. The castle is bizarre. Besides having this dungeon, it's filled with clocks.'

'You must feel right at home,' Adam remarked.

'There's something funny about these clocks. They all run backward.'

'That's interesting. We followed you here by walking towards the tombstone backward.'

Watch nodded. 'That's the key. That's the answer to the riddle.'

'But when we tried to go back through the tombstone the same way, nothing happened.'

'You tried to go back? You were just going to leave me here?'

'We took one look and figured you were as good as dead.'

Watch was understanding. 'I would probably have done the same thing.' His head suddenly twisted to one side. 'I think she's coming.'

Fourteen

It was not one figure, but several, who appeared through a large iron door at the end of the dark corridor. The black knight led the way, the metal soles of his boots ringing on the hard floor with a sound all too familiar to Adam. Behind him stumbled three kids, girls, all chained together. The first was missing her mouth, the second her eyes, the third her ears. But where the parts had been removed was not gory and gross. Rather, each of the girls looked as if she had been sewn up like a doll. Where the parts had been removed there was just skin.

Behind them all strode the witch.

It was Ann Templeton – and it was not.

Her face was the same, but, as Watch had remarked, her hair was red instead of black. It flowed down her back, moving like liquid fire over her seamless black cape. Also, the way she held herself was different from that of the woman he had met earlier in the day. Ann Templeton had seemed easy-going, possessed of a wicked sense of humour, true, but not scary. A pale light shone from this woman's face. Her eyes, although green like her interdimensional sister's, glittered like emeralds. She certainly didn't look like the mother type.

Across from them, the three deformed girls were thrown into a cramped prison and chained to the wall, where they huddled together, broken. The witch stopped in front of Watch and Adam's cell, the black knight at her side. For a long time she stared at them both, her eyes finally coming to rest on Adam. A faint smile touched her lips, as cold as her eyes.

'Are you enjoying Spooksville?' she asked. 'Seen all the sights?'

Adam had to remember to breathe. 'It's very nice, ma'am.'

Her smile widened. 'I'm glad you approve. But tomorrow it might not look the same to you. It might look very black indeed.'

Adam realised she was talking about removing his eyes. 'But, ma'am,' he stuttered. 'Remember how I saved your car from the shopping trolley? You said to me, "Thank you, Adam. You have done your good deed for the day." ' He added weakly, 'I thought you were my friend.'

She threw back her head and laughed. 'You mistake me for someone else. But that mistake is understandable. All the mirrors in this castle are dusty. One reflection can look much like another.' She moved closer to the bars that separated them and put a hand on the metal. Adam saw that she wore a ruby ring on her right hand. The interior of the stone burned with a wickless flame. 'I am not Ann Templeton, although I know her well. The skeletons you found in that house do not belong to your parents, although they might in the future. But none of that should concern you now. You are about to enter eternal darkness. You have only one chance to escape. That is to tell me where your friend Sally is hiding.'

Sally must have escaped, Adam realised. He was happy for that at least. He stood proudly as the witch waited for his response. The chain held him close to the wall.

'I don't know where she is,' he said. 'But if I did, I wouldn't tell you. Not even if you threatened to boil me in a pot of water.'

'You don't want to emphasise the pot of boiling water,' Watch muttered.

The witch smiled again, this time maybe a little sadly. 'You have such beautiful eyes, Adam. They look so nice where they are.' Her voice hardened. 'But I suppose they will look nice on one of my dolls.' She raised her hand

and snapped her fingers. 'Take them upstairs. We will not wait until tomorrow to operate.'

The black knight drew his sword and stepped forward.

Fifteen

Chained together, Adam and Watch were dragged up a long stone stairway to what appeared to be the living-room of the castle – if castles have living-rooms. It was a place of shadows, of candles that burned with red flames, and of paintings with eyes that moved. The dark ceiling, high above their heads, was all but invisible. While the witch watched, the knight chained them to an iron post in one corner of the room.

All around them, as Watch had said, were clocks that ran backward.

And there was something else. Something that appeared to be magical.

In the centre of the room, on a silver pedestal, was an hour-glass. Tall as a man, it was wrought of polished gold and burning jewels. The sand that poured through its narrow neck sparkled like diamond chips.

Not only that. The sand flowed from the bottom of the hour-glass to the top.

The witch noticed his interest in the hour-glass.

She smiled. 'In your world there is a fable about a girl who walked through a mirror and ended up in a magical land. The same principle applies here. Only you walked into a tombstone and ended up in a place of black magic. But you might be surprised to know that there also exists an hour-glass like this in your Spooksville. There the sand flows down and time moves forward. Do you understand?'

'Yes,' Adam said. 'And here the sand flows up and time moves backward.'

She nodded her approval. 'But for you now it will stop. Without eyes, without day and night, time moves very slowly.' She took a step towards them. 'This is your last chance, Adam. Tell me where Sally is and I will let you go.'

'Don't you want to give me a last chance?' Watch asked.

'Shut your mouth,' the witch said. 'While you still can. In a few minutes you won't have one to shut.'

'You give me your word you'll let me go?' Adam asked.

'Of course,' she said.

'The promise of a witch is useless,' Watch said. 'They're all liars.'

'Are you just saying that because she isn't giving you a last chance?' Adam asked.

'Maybe,' Watch admitted.

Adam considered a moment. 'You won't let me go,' he finally said. 'The moment you have Sally, you'll cut my eyes out. You may as well take them now and save us both a lot of trouble.'

A flash of anger crossed the witch's face. But then she smiled and reached out and touched his chin with her long fingernails.

'It is no trouble for me to take my time with you,' she said softly. 'And since you mentioned a pot of boiling water, I think I will have you take a bath before your operation. An especially hot one, one that will melt off your skin. What do you think of that?'

Adam swallowed. 'I prefer showers to baths.'

The witch laughed and glanced at the knight. 'Come, we must get everything ready for our brave boys.' She scratched Adam's chin, drawing a drop of blood, just before she withdrew her arm and turned away. 'We'll see how brave they are when they start screaming.'

Watch spoke up. 'I don't like baths or showers, ma'am.'

'You have no choice in the matter,' the witch called over her shoulder as she strode away, the black knight following her. They disappeared into another room.

Adam apologised to Watch. 'Sorry about volunteering you for the boiling pot.'

Watch shrugged. 'There could be worse things.'

'Such as?'

Watch frowned. 'I can't think of anything worse at the moment.' He nodded to the hour-glass. 'That's a fancy piece of magic there. The witch made a big deal of it. I wonder if it actually controls the movement of time in this dimension.'

'I wondered the same thing,' Adam said.

A minute of strained silence settled between them.

'What are we going to do now?' Watch finally asked.

'You don't have any brilliant ideas?'

'No. Do you?'

Adam yanked at the chain that bound them. 'No. It looks like this is the end.'

Watch pulled at his chains, getting nowhere. 'It does look hopeless. Sorry I talked you into taking the Secret Path. It wasn't the best introduction to Spooksville.'

'That's all right. It wasn't your fault. I wanted to go.' Adam sighed, feeling tears fill his eyes. 'I would just feel a little better knowing that Sally was safe.'

A voice spoke above and behind them.

'Isn't that sweet,' Sally said.

Sixteen

Sally was peering in through a barred window approximately twenty feet above their heads. She was dirty and tired-looking but otherwise no worse for wear.

'Sally!' Adam cried. 'What are you doing here?'

'I'm trying to rescue you guys,' she explained. 'But I haven't found a way inside this stone house.'

'You should get out of here,' Adam said. 'We're doomed. Save yourself.'

Watch cleared his throat. 'Excuse me. I wouldn't mind getting rescued.'

Adam considered. 'You're right. If she can save us without getting caught, that might not be a bad idea.' He turned back to Sally. 'Can't you crawl in through those bars? They look far enough apart.'

'Oh, I can crawl through the bars all right,' she said.

'But then what am I supposed to do? Fly down to you guys?'

Watch nodded above their heads. 'There's that chandelier there. You might be able to jump and catch hold of it.'

'It isn't that far from the window ledge,' Adam agreed.

'Who do you think I am?' Sally demanded. 'Tarzan? I can't swing from a chandelier. I might get hurt.'

'That's true,' Watch said. 'But we're about to be boiled to death. I think the time for caution has passed.'

'I agree,' Adam said.

'I thought you were worried about my safety,' Sally said indignantly.

'I am,' Adam said quickly. 'I'm just—'

'More worried about my own safety,' Watch interrupted.

'I didn't say that,' Adam said.

'You were thinking it,' Watch said. He glanced at one of his watches. 'If you are going to try to rescue us, you'd better do it now. The witch and her black knight will be back any second.'

Sally squirmed through the metal bars – getting stuck only once – and crouched on the stone window ledge. She eyed the chandelier – which had candles instead of electric lights – warily. It was only six feet away, but from her perspective, it was a huge six feet.

'What if I miss and go splat on the ground?' she asked.

'It won't be as painful as being boiled,' Adam said.

'What am I supposed to do once I'm swinging from the chandelier?' she asked.

'We'll worry about that if you make it that far,' Watch said.

'Somehow,' Sally said, 'you guys don't fit the hero mode.' She braced herself. 'I'm going to do it. One – two – three.'

Sally leaped. Her outstretched fingers barely reached the rim of the chandelier. The shock of added weight immediately pulled down on the rope that suspended the chandelier from the ceiling, which wasn't such a bad thing. Like Tarzan or Jane, Sally was able to ride the sinking chandelier all the way to the floor. The candles toppled and went out, their blood-coloured wax spilling everywhere. Luckily candles in the wall sconces still burned. When Sally was safely on her feet, she casually brushed herself off and walked over to them.

'Did you know,' she said, 'that this castle is surrounded by a moat filled with crocodiles and alligators?'

'We'll worry about them if we get that far,' Watch repeated. He gestured to their chains. 'I don't suppose you have the key to these in your pocket?'

'Can't say I do,' Sally said, glancing round. 'Where's the witch?'

'Filling our bath,' Adam said. He glanced at Watch. 'We have to face the fact we aren't going to be able to break these chains. But what if we have Sally break something else?'

'What?' they both asked.

Adam nodded to the hour-glass. 'It's her pride and joy. Most witches have a black cat, but she's got that. Maybe it's the source of her power. Knock it over, Sally. Break the glass and spread the dust over the floor.'

The idea of destruction appealed to Sally right then. Or so Adam supposed as he watched her attack the hour-glass as if she was a hungry lion jumping a plump zebra. The thing was not welded down. The witch had probably never had an unchained guest who hated hour-glasses. A few stiff kicks and the thing fell over. It hit the floor with tremendous force. The glass walls ruptured. The diamond dust flew across the stone floor.

Then everything in the nightmarish realm went crazy.

The candles in the wall sconces flickered, almost going out, which would have plunged the room into total darkness. The ground shook as if gripped by an earthquake. The noise was incredible. The castle's stone walls began to crack, the dust from the splintering stones showered down on them. But best of all, the iron pole around which Adam and Watch were bound cracked in two. They were able to pull their wristbands up and over the pole. Deep in a lower room, they heard the witch howl in anger.

'We'd better get out of here quick,' Adam said, grabbing hold of Sally, his hands still somewhat tied by the handcuffs. 'She sounds unhappy.'

'That's putting it mildly,' Watch remarked, straightening his glasses. They raced towards what they hoped was the front door. Then Adam stopped them.

'Wait a second,' he said. 'We can't just leave the others in the dungeon.'

'What others?' Sally demanded as the ground continued to rock. It was as if the castle was being ripped apart by the seams.

'There's a bunch of kids in the dungeon,' Watch explained. 'They seem nice.' He added, 'They're just missing a few parts.'

Sally made a face. 'I do hope they have plastic surgeons in this dimension.'

'We have to get them out before the whole castle caves in,' Adam said.

Sally and Watch looked at each other. 'He's really into this hero thing all of a sudden,' she said.

'We should never have called him a coward,' Watch agreed.

Adam was impatient. 'I'm going back for them.'

Sally didn't protest. 'We may as well. All we have waiting for us outside this door is a bunch of hungry crocodiles and alligators.'

Just before they left the living-room, Adam stooped and picked up a handful of the diamond dust that had fallen from the cracked hour-glass. It sparkled in his hands like a million tiny suns. Like magic, really. He stuffed it in his pockets.

Running, they found the door to the dungeon and hurried down the winding stairway. But when they reached the dungeon, they discovered that all the cells had burst open. The prisoners had already escaped.

'But where did they go?' Adam wondered aloud.

'This hallway must lead to a way out,' Watch said, nodding ahead. 'Or at least it must lead to one now. I feel a draft of air.'

'I would rather go under the moat than try to swim across it,' Sally said.

'How did you get across in the first place?' Adam asked.

'I told the guard I was a personal friend of the witch and that I had an appointment.' Sally shrugged. 'He was a troll. He was pretty stupid. He lowered the drawbridge for me.'

The ground convulsed again. All three of them were almost thrown to the floor. Behind them the stairway collapsed in a pile of rubble. Adam helped Sally regain her balance.

'That decides it,' Adam said. 'We have to go the way the others went. It's probably the smart thing. They know this castle better than we do.'

'Yeah, but half of them are blind,' Watch remarked. Yet they had no choice and he knew it.

They raced forward, down the dark underground hallway. Up ahead, they could feel fresh air.

Behind them, they could hear the witch. Her echoing cries. Cursing them.

Seventeen

The passageway emptied into the cemetery. That was both good and bad. Good because they had to get to the cemetery if they were to escape through the interdimensional portal. Bad because the remaining corpses under the ground were climbing to the surface now that the world was coming to an end. As they ran towards the tombstone, a bony hand clawed up out of the mud and grabbed Sally's ankle.

'Help!' she cried as the hand began to pull her under.

Adam and Watch leaped to her aid. Unfortunately, the skeleton had lost none of its strength with the loss of its muscle tissue. He was one strong corpse. They couldn't pry Sally free. Her right leg vanished up to her knee and she became frantic. Adam took hold of her arms and felt himself being pulled under.

'Don't let go of me!' she pleaded.

'I won't,' Adam promised. 'Watch!'

'What?'

'Do something!' Adam said.

'Like what?' Watch asked.

'Get one of those sticks,' Adam ordered, referring to the dead branches lying around. 'Jam it between Sally's leg and the skeleton hand. It might confuse the thing.'

'I'm not that skinny,' Sally said, fighting hard to stay on the surface. Slowly, steadily, Adam was losing his battle with the unseen monster. A few more seconds and Sally would be in a coffin.

'Hurry!' Adam snapped at Watch.

Watch found a suitably strong stick and stuck it down into the hole that had widened as more and more of Sally's body disappeared into it. But because he was working in the dark and in the mud, Watch had trouble wedging the stick between the hand and Sally's ankle. Finally he found his mark. Sally let out a scream. Watch was, after all, using her calf bone as leverage.

'That hurts!' she complained.

'Getting chewed on hurts more,' Adam said.

'Getting boiled hurts more,' Sally said sarcastically. 'I've heard it all before.' She slapped Watch on the back as he struggled with the subterranean creature. 'Just get this thing to let go of me!'

'It would help if you didn't disturb my concentration,' Watch said.

Sally slipped deeper into the hole and Adam almost lost his grip. 'Adam!' she cried desperately.

'Sally!' he cried back.

'If you love me,' she pleaded, 'stick your own leg in the hole. Maybe it will go for you instead of me.'

'He doesn't love you that much,' Watch muttered when Adam made no move to offer his leg. Watch continued, 'Just hold on a few seconds more. I think – Yes! It's taking the bait! It's grabbed the stick. Pull your leg out, Sally!'

'Gladly!' she cried in relief. The moment the creature let go of her, Adam was able to yank Sally free. He helped brush the earth off her as she stood up. She pushed away his hands.

'The last thing I'm worried about right now is how I look,' she said. She pointed to the tombstone. 'How do we get through that thing?'

'We better figure that out quick,' Watch said, glancing over his shoulder in the direction of the toppling castle. 'We have company.'

It was true. The black knight was coming.

And with him the witch.

Eighteen

They hurried toward the tombstone, backwards. But all they got for their troubles were more bruises on the back of their heads. The interdimensional portal was not open.

'Why isn't it working?' Sally demanded.

'I suppose you could ask the witch,' Adam muttered. 'She'll be here in a minute.'

'The knight will be here before her,' Watch said grimly, pointing. 'Look, he's coming round that tree. We need weapons. A few strong sticks.'

'A few hand phasers would be better,' Sally remarked.

They quickly scavenged for sturdy branches that they could use as oversized batons. In a rough semicircle they stood guard in front of the tombstone. The knight approached warily, his silver sword drawn. Behind him, maybe two hundred yards, the witch strode rapidly through the convulsing graveyard. Her hair shone like flames. The

111

light in her green eyes was the sickly colour of death. When the knight was maybe twenty feet away, Adam ordered the others to spread out around him.

'We'll come at him from every side,' he said.

They fanned out. The knight, although big and strong, was somewhat clumsy. Adam smacked his steelplated knee with his wooden stick and the knight almost lost his balance. Sally was more bold. Coming at him from behind, she whacked the knight over the top of the head. He didn't like that.

In a surprisingly swift move, the knight pivoted.

He swung at Sally with his silver sword.

Watch and Adam gasped.

Fortunately, Sally ducked.

The knight's stroke missed. For a moment he stumbled. Watch took the opportunity to drop his stick and leap on to the knight's back. His arms flew round the knight's neck and he rode the black warrior as he would a galloping horse.

'What are you doing?' Adam cried.

'I saw this in a movie!' Watch called back, barely able to hold on to the knight.

'We have to get him off there!' Sally cried, rushing to Adam's side. 'The knight will kill him.'

No truer words were ever spoken. Even though they

could whack the knight with their poles, they couldn't rush him directly. Not unless they wanted to be cut down by his sword. Adam and Sally watched helplessly as the knight reached over his shoulder and grabbed Watch by the arm. Slowly he began to pull Watch to the front, raising his sword in the process. In a moment, Adam knew, Watch would be missing his head.

Just then a bony hand stabbed out of the ground.

Twirling dead fingers searched left and right. As if worked by invisible radar, the skeleton's palm scanned the area. Struggling with Watch, the knight stepped one step too close to it.

The hand grabbed the knight's boot.

The knight dropped Watch and stared down at the thing.

Making an angry noise, the knight raised his silver sword.

The skeleton yanked hard on the black boot.

The knight lost his balance and fell backward, dropping his sword.

Another skeleton arm wrapped round the knight's neck.

He was being pulled under.

Adam, Sally and Watch let out a shout of victory.

For about two seconds.

'Enjoying yourselves?' the witch asked, standing dangerously tall, only thirty feet away. In the struggle with the knight, they had momentarily forgotten her. The fire in her ruby ring flared and a cold green light shone in her eyes. She took a step forward and smiled wickedly. 'You have been more trouble than I expected. But at least now I have the three of you together.'

Adam reached for the knight's sword. It was incredibly heavy. Motioning the others behind him, he pointed the sharp blade at the witch.

'Take another step,' he warned, 'and I'll run you through.'

'Ha!' the witch said, and took another step forward, moving between them and the tombstone. 'You would be no match for me if you had a hundred men and a hundred swords behind you.' She raised her right hand, the one that held the burning ring. 'This second I could melt you as if you were made of wax.'

'I think she's serious,' Sally observed.

'Perhaps we could discuss terms of surrender,' Watch said.

'No,' Adam said. 'You don't want to bargain with a witch. And maybe we don't have to. Something just occurred to me. The clocks run backwards here. Time moves backwards. Everything here is backwards. Maybe walking forwards here is the same as walking backwards at home.'

'Huh?' Sally said.

'We should go through the tombstone straight on!' Watch said excitedly.

'Exactly,' Adam said.

'Why did you have to think of that now that the witch is blocking our way?' Sally asked.

The witch mocked them as she moved directly in front of the tombstone. 'Yes, Adam, your brilliant idea came a few seconds too late,' she said. 'Now what are you going to do? Search for another witch's tombstone? I'm afraid the only way you can find another is if you kill me and erect a stone over my grave.' Her left hand caressed the ring on her right hand. The fire within the jewel continued to grow. Her smile broadened as she added, 'A blind boy might find that hard to do, don't you think?'

Adam was sick and tired of her threats.

'I'm not blind yet!' he cried, and rushed at her with the sword.

Unfortunately, he didn't get too far.

A tongue of flame leaped out from the glowing ruby. It struck the tip of the sword, and licked down the shaft of the blade. Feeling his hand burning, Adam dropped the sword to the ground. At his feet the knight's weapon melted into a silver puddle. Adam stared at it for a moment, amazed. He didn't even see the witch reach over and grab him by the throat. But he saw her eyes, oh yes, as she pulled his face up to hers. Her green eyes shone like lasers, and he had to blink to see. Out of the corner of his eye, he saw the sharp nail on her free hand approach.

'I think I will gouge out your eyes here and now,' the witch said grimly. 'In front of your friends. Let them have a good look at what becomes of those who defy me.'

'Just one second!' Adam pleaded. 'I have something for you. I stole it from your castle.'

The witch paused, her sharp nails now only inches from his face. 'What did you steal from my castle?' she demanded.

'I'll show you,' Adam replied.

He reached in his pocket and pulled out a handful of the dust from the hour-glass.

The diamond dust. The magic stuff.

He opened his palm and held it in front of her face.

The witch stared at it, shocked.

'You will pay for what you did to my clock,' she swore.

'Sure,' Adam said. 'But not today.'

Adam took a deep breath and blew the dust in her eyes.

The witch screamed and dropped him. Staggering back, rubbing her now burning eyes, she tripped over the head of the black knight – which was all that was visible of the poor guy. Letting out another bitter cry, the witch fell to the ground. Bony hands thrust up through the soil and grabbed her by her red hair. They pulled hard, and the witch began to go under.

Adam did not wait to see if she was able to break free.

'Come on!' he shouted to the others.

Holding hands, with Sally in the middle, they leaped towards the tombstone.

The world spun, the universe turned. The earth became the sky and the sky became the ocean. They fell without moving. They flew without wings. Finally everything went black and time seemed to stop.

Then they were standing on the other side of the tombstone.

A blue sky shone overhead.

They were home. Safe in Spooksville.

Epilogue

Adam walked Sally home. Watch had gone off to buy another turkey sandwich and talk to Bum. Watch wanted to know if there was another Secret Path. As if the first one had not been enough for one day. Adam and Sally wished him good luck.

'Take your glasses with you this time,' Adam had told him. 'I'm not bringing them to you again.'

As they walked the peaceful streets of the *real* Spooksville, they both noticed that the sun was almost directly overhead.

'It looks like the same time of day as when we met,' Sally said.

'It probably is,' Adam said. 'I think the whole time we were on the other side, we were moving backwards in time. I wouldn't be surprised if we run into ourselves leaving my house.' He paused. 'Maybe we should hurry and stop ourselves. Save ourselves all the trouble.'

'Why? Let them enjoy the adventure.'

Adam was amazed. 'You enjoyed today?'

'Sure. Just another day in Spooksville. You'll get used to Sundays like this.'

Adam felt exhausted. 'I hope not.'

They said goodbye at the end of Sally's driveway.

'I would invite you in,' she said. 'Except my parents are kind of weird.'

'That's OK. I'd better get home and help my dad unpack the truck.'

Sally leaned closer and stared into his eyes. 'I like you, Adam.'

He felt nervous. 'I like you.'

'Could you tell me something? Please?'

'What?'

'What was her name?' Sally asked.

'Whose name?'

'The girl you left behind.'

'I didn't leave any girl behind. I told you.'

'You were serious?' Sally said.

'I was and I am.'

'I don't have to be jealous?'

Adam had to laugh. 'You don't have to be jealous, Sally. I promise.'

'That's a relief.' She smiled and squeezed his shoulder. 'Will I see you soon?'

Adam shrugged. 'Probably tomorrow.'

Adam walked home. His parents and sister were in the kitchen, still eating lunch.

'Back so soon?' his dad asked.

Adam tried not to smirk. 'Yeah,' he said. 'How's your back?'

'Fine,' his dad said.

'What's the town like?' his mother asked.

'It's interesting.' Adam thought for a moment. 'I don't think I'm going to be bored here.'

Spooksville

The Howling Ghost

Cindy's younger brother, Neil, has disappeared. She knows a ghost has abducted him, but nobody will believe her.

Nobody, that is, except Sally. Sally believes in ghosts, and she knows they are a dime a dozen in Spooksville. So, with Adam and Watch, she tries to rescue Neil.

But this a nasty ghost. It hates *living* kids . . .

Spooksville

The Haunted Cave

There's a famous cave outside Spooksville. Adam, Sally, Watch and Cindy can't wait to explore it. But that's a big mistake.

The moment they enter the cave, the entrance closes behind them.

They're trapped in darkness.

Then they realise that something is following them. Something big, black and very hungry . . .

Exclusive watch for

Spooksville

fans!

Even Watch would be pleased to add this fantastic bubble watch to his collection! It's a digital time keeper with a difference! For one thing there's a special Spooksville bat floating around inside!

*The watch is totally exclusive and can be yours for only **£4.99** (incl. post and packing*

TAKE ADVANTAGE OF THIS SPECIAL OFFER. COLLECT SIX SPECIAL TOKENS AND CLAIM THE WATCH ABSOLUTELY FREE. COLLECT THREE TOKENS AND GET THE WATCH FOR ONLY £2.5

*You'll find the tokens in special editions of Spooksville.
Look for the flash on the cover*

PLEASE ALLOW 28 DAYS FOR DELIVERY.

Enclose a cheque/postal order payable to *Spooksville Watch Promotion* for £4.99 with 1 token or £2.50 with 3 tokens. Please write your name and address on the back of your cheque/postal order. Send to: SPOOKSVILLE WATCH PROMOTION, DEPT NO 648T, PO BOX 143, AYLESBURY, BUCKS HP19 3XY PLEASE NOTE this price applies to UK address **only**. Please see below for other areas:

AUSTRALIA Please send a cheque/postal order for $12.95 with 1 token or for $6.95 with 3 tokens to: SPOOKSVILLE WATCH PROMOTION, CHILDREN'S PRODUCT MANAGER, LOCKED BAG 386, RYDALMERE NSW 2116

EIRE Please send a cheque/postal order for IEP £4.99 with 1 token or IEP £2.50 with 3 tokens to: SPOOKSVILLE WATCH PROMOTION, DEPT NO 653T, PO BOX 143, AYLESBURY, BUCKS HP19 3XY

Don't forget to attach the special tokens to your cheque or postal order.

IF YOU'VE COLLECTED 6 TOKENS SEND NO MONEY AT ALL - THE WATCH IS ABSOLUTELY FREE

THIS OFFER IS AVAILABLE TO RESIDENTS OF THE UK, EIRE AND AUSTRALIA ONLY. THE CLOSING DATE IS 30TH SEPTEMBER 1997

SEE INSIDE FOR DETAILS